# HAPPY BIRTHDAY TO ME!

## Kids Pick the Funniest Birthday Poems

**by Bruce Lansky and friends**

Illustrated by
**Jack Lindstrom**

**Meadowbrook Press**
Distributed by Simon & Schuster
New York

Library of Congress Cataloging-in-Publication Data
Happy birthday to me! / by Bruce Lansky and friends : illustrated by Jack Lindstrom.
    p.  cm.
    Includes index.
    Summary: A collection of poems about birthdays, by such authors as Bruce Lansky, Dr. Seuss, and Leslie Danford Perkins.
    ISBN 0-671-58062-0 (Simon & Schuster)
    ISBN 0-88166-305-0 (Meadowbrook)
    1. Birthdays—Juvenile poetry. 2. Children's poetry, American. [1. Birthdays—Poetry.
    2. American Poetry—Collections.]
    I. Lansky, Bruce. II. Lindstrom, Jack, ill.
    PS595.B57H37  1998
    811'.54080354—dc21                         97-42044
                                                       CIP

Editorial Coordinators: Michael Platzer, Jason Sanford          AC
Copyeditor: Jason Sanford
Production Manager: Joe Gagne
Production Assistant: Danielle White
Illustrator: Jack Lindstrom

Grateful acknowledgment is made to the following for permission to reprint the copyrighted material listed below:

"Happy Birthday to Me" © 1997 by Mike Artell. Used by permission of the author.

"Thank You" © 1997 by Goldie Olszynko Gryn. Used by permission of the author.

"Dear Aunt Francis" © 1997 by Marilyn Helmer. Used by permission of the author.

"You're Invited to (Name's) Party!" "On the Day That You Were Born," "What You Were Like When You Were Born," "Today Is Your Lucky Day," "Birthday Wishes," "Birthday Predictions," "Birthday Roast," "Birthday Advice," "Birthday Rules," "Act Your Age," "Canceled Until Further Notice," "Blow Harder!" and "Miss Suzy's Birthday" © 1997 by Bruce Lansky. "Happy Birthday from Your Loving Brother" © 1996 by Bruce Lansky. All poems used by permission of the author.

"Creative Cooking" © 1997 by Leslie Danford Perkins. Used by permission of the author.

"The Revenge of the Birthday Aunts" © 1997 by Michael Platzer. Used by permission of the author

"When Frankenstein Came to My Birthday" © 1997 by Robert Scotellaro. Used by permission of the author.

"If We Didn't Have Birthdays" from Happy Birthday to You! by Dr. Seuss TM and copyright © 1959 and renewed 1987 by Dr. Seuss Enterprises, L.P. Reprinted by permission of Random House, Inc.

Published by Meadowbrook Press, 5451 Smetana Drive, Minnetonka, MN 55343

BOOK TRADE DISTRIBUTION by Simon & Schuster, a division on Simon and Schuster, Inc., 1230 Avenue of the Americas, New York, NY 10020

02 01 00 99 98        10 9 8 7 6 5 4 3 2 1

Printed in the United States of America

# CONTENTS

# You're Invited to _____ Party!
(Name's)

On the _____ of _____,
   (date)     (month)
please write down the date,

here's a party for _____
             (name)
that's going to be great.

The fun will be starting

at _____ on the dot.
 (hour)
It runs to _____.
    (hour)
An all nighter it's not.

The dress code is casual,

so you can have fun.

There'll be _____ and _____
      (activity)       (activity)
to please everyone.

Please leave room for _____.
          (meal)
The food will be great.

(We won't tell your mom

if you don't clean your plate.)

I'm so proud of _____,
        (name)
I've written this rhyme.

So, come to _____ party
    (his/her)
and have a good time.

*Bruce Lansky*

# On the Day That You Were Born

On the day that you were born,
your father was so proud.
No other baby in (his/her) crib
could scream and cry so loud.

No other baby kicked (his/her) covers
to the nursery floor.
No other baby drank (his/her) milk
then yelled, "I want some more!"

And when you messed your diapers,
nurses rang the fire bell.
Then firemen with hoses
would spray the nursery well.

You would have been so boring,
so quiet and well-bred,
if the clumsy doctor hadn't
dropped you on your head.

*Bruce Lansky*

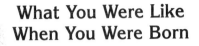

## What You Were Like When You Were Born

When you were born
you looked so cute
all dressed up in
your birthday suit.

Before you had
been home a week
we noticed that
you'd sprung a leak.

You slept all day
and cried all night—
as soon as we
turned off the light.

To keep you quiet
in your bed
we stuck a diaper
on your head.

*Bruce Lansky*

3

# If We Didn't Have Birthdays

If we didn't have birthdays, you wouldn't be you.
If you'd never been born, well then what would you do?
If you'd never been born, well then what would you be?
You *might* be a fish! Or a toad in a tree!
You might be a doorknob! Or three baked potatoes!
You might be a bag full of hard green tomatoes.
Or worse than all that . . . Why, you might be a WASN'T!
A Wasn't has no fun at all. No, he doesn't.
A Wasn't just isn't. He just isn't present.
But you . . . You ARE YOU! And, now isn't that pleasant!

*Dr. Seuss*

4

## Today Is Your Lucky Day

Today on your birthday
consider your luck.
You could have been born
as a pig, cow, or duck.

You could have been born
crying oink, quack, or moo.
You're lucky you didn't
wind up in the zoo.

*Bruce Lansky*

# Birthday Wishes

I wish for peace.
I wish for knowledge.
I wish my (brother/sister)
would leave for college.

*Bruce Lansky*

## Birthday Predictions

In twenty years you will have money.
In thirty years you will have fame.
In forty years you will have gray hair
and won't even know your own name.

*Bruce Lansky*

# Birthday Roast

We've gathered here to celebrate
the birthday of a friend.
We hope (his/her) weird behavior
will soon be at an end.

(He/She) didn't go to school today.
(He/She) missed a spelling test.
They wouldn't let (him/her) on the bus,
because (he/she) wasn't dressed.

(He/She) hasn't made (his/her) bed
or cleaned (his/her) room for several years.
We called (his/her) room a pig pen,
and (he/she) burst out into tears.

One thing about dear _____
that makes us very proud: <sup>(name)</sup>
When (he/she) throws a temper tantrum,
(he/she) always draws a crowd.

It's very clear our birthday (boy/girl)
is going through a stage.
We hope that (his/her) behavior
will catch up to (his/her) age.

*Bruce Lansky*

# Birthday Advice

Today on your birthday
I think you should know—
you're getting too old now
to suck on your toe.

And when you get hungry
I hope you won't spread
the jam that you find
'tween your toes on your bread.

Do not shine your shoes
with the wax from your ear.
Don't shampoo your hair
with your dad's favorite beer.

Do not chase your nose
when it's running—that's dumb.
When you go to church,
do not dress like a bum.

It's time you grew up
and stopped acting so bad.
It's time that you stopped
acting just like your dad.

*Bruce Lansky*

## Birthday Rules

Don't invite your friends who haven't learned to use the potty.
Changing diapers, you can bet, will drive your mother dotty.

Don't complain when Grandpa Gus gives you a birthday kiss.
If you're bothered by his beard, just dodge so he will miss.

Don't spill cake and ice cream on your sister's brand new dress.
Do not start a food fight; you will have to clean the mess.

10

Don't try to pin the donkey tail on your fat uncle Fred.
Don't ask Cousin Carla's boyfriend when they plan to wed.

If you get a gift you hate, remember not to swear.
Do not cry when Grandma gives you purple underwear.

If you follow all these rules, your birthday fun will double.
And if you disobey them, you will be in lots of trouble.

*Bruce Lansky*

11

# When Frankenstein Came to My Birthday

He came to my birthday and banged down the door.
He knocked over plates and dropped cake on the floor.
He shouted so loud that we plugged up our ears.
He stomped on our sneakers, which brought us to tears.
He drank all the punch, for he had a great thirst.
He squeezed me so tight that I thought I would burst!
He sat on the couch and it broke into bits.
My mother and father were both having fits.
"We all make mistakes," Momma said, "now and then.
But don't invite Frankenstein, ever again!!!"

*Robert Scotellaro*

13

14

# The Revenge of the Birthday Aunts

Mom planned my birthday party,
but she didn't use her brain.
She invited all my nutty aunts;
they drove me half insane.

They opened up my presents
and they gobbled down my cake.
They yapped and yammered on and on,
which made my poor head ache.

They tried to hug and kiss me,
but I shouted, "That's enough!
I can't stand one more second
of this awful auntie stuff!"

And so I sent them packing—
but I'm filled with dread and fear.
As my aunties left, they said,
"We're coming back next year."

*Michael Platzer*

# Happy Birthday to Me

Happy birthday to me.
I like what I see!
There's plenty of junk food,
and the presents are free!

*Mike Artell*

## Act Your Age

Happy birthday to you.
How could it be true?
You're supposed to be _____,
(age of birthday boy or girl)
But you act like you're two.

*Bruce Lansky*

17

## Creative Cooking

I baked my father's birthday cake.
I did it by myself.
I used my mother's cookbook
that was lying on the shelf.

The cookbook called for flour,
so I picked a yellow rose.
I washed the dirt and bugs off
with my mother's garden hose.

The cookbook called for egg whites,
so I chopped up all the shells.
I stirred them with the yellow rose,
which made delicious smells.

The baking powder can was gone,
and so I used instead
the powder Mother sprinkles
on my baby brother, Fred.

I baked the cake and then
I made some icing out of ice.
I don't know how the cake will taste,
but wow! It sure looks nice.

*Leslie Danford Perkins*

# Canceled Until Further Notice

I'm calling you up to inform you:
My birthday's been canceled today.
I'm sorry to give such short notice.
But my parents have said, "There's no way!"

I'm sorry to cause you such trouble.
I made such a stupid mistake.
Last night when I should have been sleeping,
I ate up my whole birthday cake.

So, don't bother coming to see me.
I'm grounded. My room is my jail.
And now that I've told you I'm sorry,
please send me my present by mail.

*Bruce Lansky*

21

## Blow Harder!

If you can't blow the candles out,
your wish will not come true.
Don't worry, just be glad that you're not
turning ninety-two.

*Bruce Lansky*

# Miss Suzy's Birthday

Miss Suzy had a birthday.
It wasn't any fun.
She couldn't blow the candles out,
'cause she was only one.

She dribbled on the candles.
She dribbled on the cake.
Miss Suzy had to eat it all
and got a tummy ache.

She yelled and screamed all evening.
She cried the whole night through.
She never got another cake
till she was twenty-two.

*Bruce Lansky*

## Thank You

Thank you for the birthday cake
(it tasted like my socks).
Thank you for the birthday gift
(at least I liked the box).
Thank you for the birthday song
(you yelled into my ear).
Thank you for the birthday punch
(left over from last year).
Thank you, Mom, and thank you, Dad,
and thank you, Brother Ben.
I'll thank you now for never ever
doing this again!

*Goldie Olszynko Gryn*

24

# Happy Birthday
# from Your Loving Brother

My sister plays with Barbie dolls.
She likes to wear a skirt.
Her room's so neat and tidy that
I think she's scared of dirt.

I know I cannot change her.
But I love to see her squirm.
And so on her next birthday
I am giving her a worm.

*Bruce Lansky*

OPEN
ME
FIRST!

25

# Dear Aunt Francis

Dear Aunt Francis:

Thank you for the finger paints.
I like your gift so much!
I've painted everything in sight.
I've got the artist's touch.

I've painted murals on the walls,
I've painted my dog, Rover,
Mom's exercycle, Dad's new shoes.
I've still got paint left over.

And here's good news, Aunt Francis.
Mom says that I can stay
at your house any time I want
and finger-paint all day!

      See you real soon,
           Your loving nephew,
               Vincent

*Marilyn Helmer*

27

# TITLE INDEX

# ACKNOWLEDGMENTS

We would like to thank the more than one hundred teachers and their students who helped us select the poems for this book. Although we cannot possibly mention everyone, here is a brief list of teachers who helped us make the final selections:

Shirley Hallquist, Pinewood Elementary School; Jane Hesslein, Sunset Hill Elementary School; Carol Larson, Mississippi Elementary; Jeanne M. Nelsen, St. Mary's Catholic School; Barb Rannigan, Alta Vista Elementary School; Ron Sangalang, Sherwood Forest Elementary School; Mary Jane Savaiano, Clara Barton Open School; Suzanne Thompson, Holy Name of Jesus Catholic School; Timothy Tocher, George Grant Mason Elementary; and Lynette Townsend, Lomarena Elementary School.